DATE DUE

HOLLY KELLER

ten sleepy sheep

Greenwillow Books   New York

Library of Congress Cataloging in Publication Data
Keller, Holly.
Ten sleepy sheep.
Summary: Lewis counts sheep to help him
sleep, but he soon finds ten noisy sheep
having a party in his bedroom.
[1. Bedtime—Fiction. 2. Counting.
3. Sheep—Fiction] I. Title.
PZ7.K28132Te 1983   [E]   83-1477
ISBN 0-688-02306-1
ISBN 0-688-02307-X (lib. bdg.)

FOR COREY AND JESSE

One night when Lewis couldn't sleep,
Papa brought him a glass of water.

Mama read him a story,

and Grandma sang him a song.

But Lewis was as wide awake as ever.

So Grandpa tucked him back in bed
and said, "Count sheep."

The first sheep had a red balloon.

The second had a drum.

Three and four jumped through a hoop,

and five played an old tin horn.

The sixth sheep carried a plate of cookies.

The seventh had some streamers.

Eight and nine brought a bowl of punch,

and ten came blowing bubbles.

Lewis's room was full of sheep.

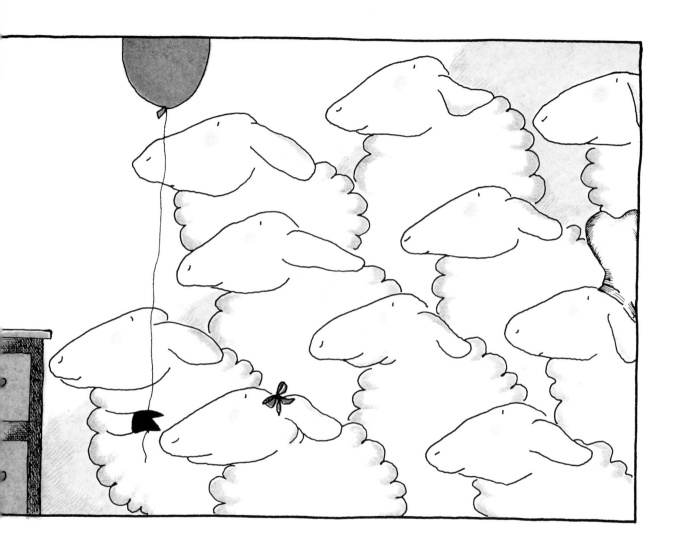

They danced around his bed and had a party.

"Please!" Lewis shouted.
"I'm trying to sleep!"
But the sheep were making
too much noise to hear.

So one by one Lewis picked them up

and put them into bed.

He brought each one a glass of water,

read them a story, and sang them a song.
Soon the sheep were all asleep.

There was nothing more to do.

So Lewis climbed in beside them

and went to sleep too.